The Three Musketeers

The Three Musketeers

by Alexandre Dumas
adapted by Deborah Felder

A STEPPING STONE BOOK™
Random House New York

 Published in the United States by Random House Children's Books, a division of Random House, Inc., New York, and simultaneously in Canada by Random House of Canada Limited, Toronto.

www.steppingstonesbooks.com
www.randomhouse.com/kids

Library of Congress Cataloging-in-Publication Data
Felder, Deborah G.
The three musketeers / by Alexandre Dumas ; adapted by Deborah Felder ; [cover illustration by Daniel Andreasen].
p. cm.
"A Stepping Stone book."
SUMMARY: In seventeenth-century France, young d'Artagnan initially quarrels with, then befriends, three musketeers and joins them in trying to outwit the enemies of the king and queen.
ISBN 0-679-86017-7 (pbk.) — ISBN 0-679-99436-X (lib. bdg.)
1. France—History—Louis XIII, 1610–1643—Juvenile fiction. [1. France—History—Louis XIII, 1610–1643—Fiction. 2. Adventure and adventurers—Fiction.]
I. Andreasen, Dan, ill. II. Dumas, Alexandre, 1802–1870. Trois mousquetaires. III. Title.
PZ7.F3356Th 2005 [Fic]—dc22 2004012327

Printed in the United States of America 21 20 19

Contents

CHAPTER 1

THE MAN WITH THE SCAR

One April morning in 1625, a young man came riding into the small town of Meung. The young man's name was d'Artagnan of Gascony. He was on his way to Paris to become one of the king's musketeers. The musketeers were the bold, brave soldiers who guarded King Louis of France.

His father's sword was buckled around d'Artagnan's waist. D'Artagnan also carried three more gifts from his father. One was a purse containing fifteen gold pieces. The second was a letter of introduction to Monsieur de Tréville, the captain of the musketeers. The third gift was the horse d'Artagnan was riding.

The citizens of Meung stared at the old, small horse. It had a yellow coat and a tail with almost no hair. It walked with its head below its knees. But d'Artagnan sat on its back proudly as he rode through the town.

He stopped at the Inn of the Honest Miller and climbed down from his horse. Three men were standing near the door. They looked at d'Artagnan and his horse and burst into laughter.

D'Artagnan's face grew warm with anger. He walked toward the men, one hand on the hilt of his sword.

"You there!" he called out. "Tell me what you're laughing at, so we can laugh together!"

The tallest of the three men turned to face d'Artagnan. He was a dark-haired nobleman with a pale face and a scar on his forehead.

"I'm not speaking to you, sir," he said with a sneer.

"But *I* am speaking to *you*!" cried d'Artagnan.

The nobleman paid no attention to d'Artagnan. He pointed to the horse and whispered something to his friends. The three men laughed again.

D'Artagnan drew his sword. "You laugh at a horse because you're afraid to laugh at its master!" he cried.

"No one can tell me when to laugh," said the nobleman. "I laugh when it suits me." With that, he turned to enter the inn.

But d'Artagnan ran after him. "You've laughed at me for the last time!" he shouted. "Turn and face me, sir, or I'll run you through from behind!"

He lunged at the nobleman. The nobleman stepped back quickly. He drew his sword and stood ready to fight.

But just then his two friends came at d'Artagnan with big sticks and shovels. D'Artagnan dropped his sword. At the same moment, one of his attackers hit him on the head. D'Artagnan fell to the ground, bleeding and almost unconscious.

The innkeeper and his servants carried

d'Artagnan into the inn. The servants bandaged the young man's wound. The innkeeper quickly searched d'Artagnan's pockets. Then he went back downstairs.

The nobleman was standing by the window.

"Well, how's the young hothead?" he asked the innkeeper.

"He's unconscious now. But before he fainted, he said he would report you to Monsieur de Tréville."

"Tréville! Are you sure?"

The innkeeper nodded. "He's also carrying a letter addressed to the captain of the musketeers." He bowed to the nobleman and hurried off to the kitchen.

The nobleman turned back to the window. There was a worried frown on his face.

"Tréville may have sent that young man here to ruin our plan," he muttered. "I hope Milady arrives soon. We must finish our business before the boy sees us."

Meanwhile, d'Artagnan had come to. He sat up with a groan. Then he climbed out of bed and staggered downstairs.

He looked out the door. The nobleman was talking to a beautiful young woman. She was seated in an elegant carriage.

"The cardinal has ordered you to return to England at once, Milady," d'Artagnan heard the nobleman say.

"And what are my instructions?" asked Milady.

"You are to let the cardinal know if the Duke of Buckingham leaves London."

"I understand. But now we must both leave quickly," she said. "The least delay—such as that young man—can ruin everything."

Milady gave an order to the driver of the carriage. The driver cracked his whip, and the carriage drove off.

The nobleman leaped on his horse and galloped off toward Paris.

"Come back, coward!" cried d'Artagnan, running out the door. But he was too weak to take more than a few steps before he fainted again. The innkeeper found him, carried him upstairs, and put him in bed.

The next morning d'Artagnan felt better. He dressed and went downstairs to the kitchen. He reached into his pocket to pay the innkeeper and found only his coin purse. The letter to Monsieur de Tréville was gone.

"What have you done with my letter?" d'Artagnan asked the innkeeper angrily.

"I didn't take it, sir," the innkeeper insisted. "It was that nobleman. He stole it while you were unconscious."

"The scoundrel! Monsieur de Tréville will hear of this theft when I reach Paris!"

D'Artagnan strode out of the inn and climbed onto his little yellow horse. As he rode out of Meung, he thought about what he had overheard the day before.

The nobleman had talked about the cardinal. D'Artagnan knew the cardinal must be Cardinal Richelieu, the most powerful man in France. But why was he sending Milady to spy on the Duke of Buckingham, the prime minister of England?

"I'll find out when I get to Paris," d'Artagnan told himself. "And I'll find the nobleman with the scar, too. He hasn't seen the last of d'Artagnan of Gascony!"

CHAPTER 2

THE CAPTAIN OF THE MUSKETEERS

Later that morning, d'Artagnan arrived at Monsieur de Tréville's house in Paris. As he walked through the courtyard, he saw groups of musketeers everywhere.

D'Artagnan gazed admiringly at the dashing soldiers. Some were practicing their dueling. Others were drinking, talking, and joking. Many of the jokes seemed to be about the cardinal's guards. They were the rivals of the musketeers.

D'Artagnan reached the main door of the house. He asked a servant to announce him to Monsieur de Tréville. The servant led d'Artagnan upstairs to an office and told him to wait by the closed door. Several musketeers had already gathered there. A few minutes later, the captain of the musketeers opened the door.

"Come in, young man," said Tréville. "I'll be with you in a moment."

Then he stuck his head out the door and called, "Athos! Porthos! Aramis!"

Two musketeers left their group and followed Tréville into the office. The musketeer called Porthos was tall and heavyset. The other, named Aramis, was slender and handsome. They stood stiffly at attention. Tréville paced back and forth in front of them.

Suddenly, Tréville stopped and looked them over from head to foot. There was an angry expression on his face.

"Do you know what the cardinal has reported?" he shouted. "He said that three of my men started a riot in a tavern yesterday. The cardinal's guards had to arrest them! Don't deny that it was you. The guards recognized you and Athos...but where is Athos?"

"Sir," Aramis said sadly, "Athos is sick."

"He may have smallpox," Porthos added.

"Wounded in another riot more likely!" said Tréville. "Let me tell you something, gentlemen. I won't have my musketeers laughed at by the cardinal's guards! How could you let yourselves be arrested by them?"

"Sir," said Porthos, "this is the truth of the matter. They attacked us before we could even draw our swords. We fought well. But Athos was badly wounded in the chest and shoulder. They tried to drag us away, but we escaped."

Tréville nodded. "So the cardinal only told half the story," he said in a softer tone.

Just then, the door opened. A handsome musketeer with a pale face entered the room. He walked slowly toward Tréville.

"Athos!" cried Porthos and Aramis.

"You sent for me, sir," Athos said weakly. "What are your orders?"

"I was just going to tell your friends that I don't want you to risk your lives needlessly," said Tréville. "But I'm proud of you all. Give me your hand, my brave and loyal Athos!"

Without thinking, he reached out and grabbed Athos' hand. Athos winced in pain and turned even paler. Then he gave a low moan and fell to the floor, unconscious.

"Get a doctor!" cried Tréville. "Hurry!"

Some musketeers who had been listening at the door ran off to find a doctor. Porthos and Aramis carried their friend into the next room. Tréville hurried after them.

After a while, Tréville came back into the office. Athos had regained consciousness. The doctor had said that he would recover.

Tréville turned to face d'Artagnan. "Now then, young man. Who are you, and what did you wish to see me about?"

As soon as d'Artagnan gave his name, Tréville's face lit up.

"Your father and I fought side by side when we were young musketeers. He is my oldest friend. Now, what can I do for his son?"

"Sir," said d'Artagnan. "I came here to ask to join the musketeers. But I'm not sure I'm worthy of such an honor."

"Yes, it *is* a great honor. No one can become a musketeer until he has performed a great act of courage. But he can also serve for two years in a lower regiment to get his training."

"If only I had the letter of introduction my father wrote to you. You would see that I need no training. But the letter was stolen."

D'Artagnan told Tréville what had happened at Meung. The captain of the musketeers listened carefully.

"Tell me, d'Artagnan," said Tréville. "Did that nobleman have a scar?"

"Yes, on his forehead."

"And was he tall, with a pale face and dark hair?" asked Tréville.

"Yes, sir."

"And the woman he met—did you hear her name?"

"He called her Milady," said d'Artagnan.

"Do you know what they talked about?"

"He gave her the cardinal's orders. She was to return to England. Then she was to inform the cardinal if the Duke of Buckingham left London."

"It is he," murmured Tréville. "I didn't know he was back in France."

"Oh, sir, please tell me who this cowardly nobleman is," cried d'Artagnan. "I must have my revenge!"

"Put all thought of revenge out of your mind, my boy! He's not a coward. You can be sure of that. He's a very dangerous man."

Tréville sat down at his desk. "And now, I'll write a letter. It will admit you to one of our regiments. I'm sure you'll make a fine cadet."

While Tréville was writing, d'Artagnan looked out the window. He watched the musketeers leave the courtyard and disappear down the street. Suddenly, d'Artagnan shouted, "There he is!"

"Who?" asked Tréville, startled.

"The man who stole my letter!" cried

d'Artagnan, as he rushed out the door. "He won't escape me this time!"

CHAPTER 3

ATHOS' SHOULDER, PORTHOS' CLOAK, AND ARAMIS' HANDKERCHIEF

D'Artagnan was in a rage as he headed for the staircase. Suddenly, a musketeer came out of a door near the landing. D'Artagnan ran headlong into him. The musketeer cried out in pain.

"Excuse me. I'm in a hurry," d'Artagnan said without stopping.

He started down the stairs. But a hand grabbed his belt and he was forced to stop.

"That is no reason for you to run into me, young man," said the musketeer.

"I didn't do it on purpose, sir," d'Artagnan said, recognizing Athos. "Now please let me go."

"You're not polite, sir," said Athos.

"Well, *you're* not going to give me a lesson in manners," fumed d'Artagnan.

"No? Then perhaps I can give you a lesson in dueling!" said Athos.

"I'm ready to fight a duel with you! Just tell me where and when," said d'Artagnan.

"Behind the Carmelite convent at noon," Athos said. He let go of d'Artagnan's belt.

"I'll be there!" said d'Artagnan. He raced down the stairs.

Porthos and a soldier stood at the front door. D'Artagnan darted through the small space between the two men. But a gust of wind lifted Porthos' long velvet cloak. D'Artagnan ran straight into the cloak and became tangled inside the folds.

"Are you a wild man?" cried Porthos as d'Artagnan struggled to free himself.

D'Artagnan finally untangled himself. "Excuse me, sir," he said, looking up at the gigantic musketeer. "But I'm in a hurry."

"Do you close your eyes when you're in

a hurry? You need to be taught a lesson!"

"And who is going to teach it to me?" d'Artagnan asked angrily. "You?"

"I, sir!" cried Porthos. "Behind the Luxembourg Gardens at one o'clock!"

"At one o'clock, then," said d'Artagnan.

He dashed through the courtyard into the street. He looked around. But there was no sign of the nobleman.

"What a scatterbrained idiot I am!" he muttered to himself. "It was very rude of me to run out of Monsieur de Tréville's office like that. And now I must fight two duels with musketeers! If I survive, I will remember to be more polite in the future."

Just then, he saw Aramis talking to three guards. He bowed deeply to the musketeer. Aramis nodded at d'Artagnan and continued to talk to the guards.

D'Artagnan was about to move on. Then he saw Aramis drop his handkerchief and step on it. D'Artagnan bent down and pulled the handkerchief from under Aramis' foot.

"I believe that you have lost your handkerchief, sir," he said politely.

Aramis turned red. He grabbed the lacy handkerchief from d'Artagnan's hand. The scent of perfume filled the air.

"Aha!" cried one of the guards. "A gift from one of the queen's ladies-in-waiting, Aramis? Tell us about her."

D'Artagnan saw that he had embarrassed Aramis. "I'm sorry, sir," he said. "I hope you will excuse me."

Aramis glared at him. "I will not excuse you, sir," he said coldly. "A gentleman does not step on a handkerchief unless he is trying to hide it. Any fool knows that."

"How dare you call me a fool," cried d'Artagnan. "Draw your sword, sir!"

"Not here! Meet me at Monsieur de Tréville's house at two o'clock. I know a place where we can cross swords."

"My sword will be ready," said d'Artagnan.

It was almost noon. D'Artagnan headed for

the Carmelite convent to meet Athos.

"The duel must be fought," he told himself. "But if I am to be killed today, at least I'll be killed by a musketeer."

When d'Artagnan reached the field behind the convent, Athos was waiting for him.

"My seconds should be here any moment," said the musketeer. "They will make sure we fight a fair duel."

"I have no seconds," d'Artagnan said. "I just arrived in Paris today. But it will be an honor to cross swords with you, sir."

"Thank you," Athos said with a bow. "I'll use my left hand to fight. The wound in my right shoulder is very painful."

"Then perhaps you'll let me give you an ointment," said d'Artagnan. "My mother made it. It heals any wound in three days."

"You are very kind. If we don't kill each other in this duel, I feel sure we shall become good friends. Ah, here come my seconds now!" said Athos.

D'Artagnan turned and stared at the

musketeers. "Porthos and Aramis are your seconds?" he said in a surprised tone.

"Of course! We are always together. Everyone calls us The Three Musketeers."

Porthos and Aramis came closer and saw d'Artagnan. "What's *he* doing here?" cried Porthos.

"This is the gentleman I am to duel," said Athos.

"But I have a duel with him, too!" said Porthos.

"And so do I," said Aramis.

D'Artagnan drew his sword. "Then let us begin. On guard, Monsieur Athos!"

Just as the two swords touched, a group of the cardinal's guards came toward them. They were led by Monsieur de Jussac.

"Put away your swords quickly!" called Porthos.

But it was too late. "Stop, you musketeers!" shouted Jussac. "You're under arrest for breaking the cardinal's law against dueling!"

"There are five of them against three of

us," Athos said quietly. "But I'd rather die here than face our captain after another defeat by the guards!"

"There are four of us, not three," said d'Artagnan. "It's true that I don't wear your uniform. But I have the heart of a musketeer. And I want to prove it."

"You're a fine boy," Athos said. "What's your name?"

"D'Artagnan, sir."

"Then Athos, Porthos, Aramis, and d'Artagnan will fight together! Forward!"

The four of them lunged at the cardinal's guards. D'Artagnan found himself face to face with Jussac. He fought like a tiger. Soon he had wounded the leader of the guards.

Within minutes, the musketeers had killed two guards and wounded the third. The fourth guard surrendered.

The musketeers and d'Artagnan helped the wounded man to the convent steps. Then, arm in arm, they all marched down the street together. They greeted every musketeer they met along the way.

D'Artagnan felt proud and happy as he walked with his new friends. He was on his way to becoming a musketeer!

CHAPTER 4
A KIDNAPPING

Monsieur de Tréville soon learned of the defeat of the cardinal's guards. He scolded the three musketeers in public. But he praised them in private. The king, too, was pleased at the news. He had given Cardinal Richelieu great power. However, he also enjoyed seeing him suffer a defeat.

King Louis summoned the four friends to the palace to congratulate them.

He called them into his private room. "Come in, my brave men," the king said.

The three musketeers and d'Artagnan approached the king. They bowed deeply. The king turned toward d'Artagnan.

"So you are the young Gascon," said King Louis. "I must reward you for fighting so bravely alongside my musketeers. Here are forty pistoles."

D'Artagnan took the small bag of gold coins. "Thank you, Sire," he said, bowing.

"Thank you all, gentlemen, for your loyalty to me," said the king.

The musketeers and d'Artagnan bowed again, then left the palace. D'Artagnan asked his friends how he should spend his money. Athos suggested that he treat them all to a good dinner. Porthos urged him to hire a servant. And Aramis advised him to find a place to live.

D'Artagnan took *all* their advice. Then he settled down to the life of a cadet. He trained with his regiment and spent all his free time with the three musketeers. Soon he had spent all of his forty pistoles.

One day there was a knock at the door of d'Artagnan's room. Planchet, d'Artagnan's servant, opened the door. He showed in a short, fat man.

"I've heard that you are a brave and honest man, Monsieur," the man said.

"That is why I'm going to tell you my secret."

D'Artagnan leaned forward in his chair. "I'm listening, Monsieur," he said. "Go on."

"My wife, Constance, is a lady-in-waiting to Queen Anne. Yesterday, as she left the palace, she was kidnapped."

"Kidnapped! Do you know why?"

"Because of the queen, sir," said the man. "The queen is in love with the Duke of Buckingham. And he loves her, too."

"How do you know all this?"

"From Constance," the man said. "She also told me that the queen is very frightened. She fears the cardinal will lure the duke to Paris and trap him. Then everyone will know the queen is in love with an enemy of France. She'll be disgraced!"

"But what does that have to do with your wife's kidnapping?" asked d'Artagnan.

"The queen tells all her secrets to Constance," said the man. "I think the cardinal wants to learn those secrets."

"Do you know who kidnapped her?"

"I don't know his name. He was tall, with black hair, a pale face, and a scar on his forehead."

"Why, that's my man at Meung!" cried d'Artagnan. "Are you sure you've described the right man?"

"As sure as my name is Bonacieux," said the man.

"Bonacieux," murmured d'Artagnan. "I've heard that name before."

"It's possible, sir. I am your landlord. And if you'll help me, I'll forget all about the three months' rent you owe me."

Bonacieux took a paper from his pocket. "Here is a letter I received this morning."

D'Artagnan read it out loud: "'Do not look for your wife. She will be returned to you when she is no longer needed. Try to find her, and you will be arrested.'"

"Oh, Monsieur," cried Bonacieux. "I'm terrified of being thrown into prison. Please help me! I will forget about the rent and I'll give you fifty pistoles besides!"

"Excellent!" said d'Artagnan. "Of course

I'll help you, Monsieur Bonacieux."

Soon after Bonacieux had left, Athos, Porthos, and Aramis arrived. D'Artagnan told them about Madame Bonacieux's kidnapping and the queen's problem.

As he was finishing the story, Bonacieux burst into the room. "Save me!" he cried. "They've come to arrest me!"

Behind the landlord stood four of the cardinal's guards.

"Come in, gentlemen," called d'Artagnan. "We're all loyal to the king and the cardinal. If you've come to arrest this man, we won't stop you."

"But you promised me..." cried Bonacieux.

"We can't help you or your wife unless we stay free," whispered d'Artagnan. "If we try to stop these men, we'll be arrested, too."

The guards led Bonacieux away.

"Don't worry, d'Artagnan. You can count on us," Athos said proudly. "We'll help you save her majesty's honor. We musketeers serve the queen as well as the king."

"Thank you, my friend. Let us make our motto 'All for one, and one for all.'"

The four friends joined hands. In one voice they said, "All for one, and one for all!"

"Be very careful, my friends," said d'Artagnan. "From now on we're at war with the cardinal!"

CHAPTER 5

D'ARTAGNAN TO THE RESCUE

The cardinal's guards kept a close watch on Bonacieux's apartment. Everyone who came there was questioned.

D'Artagnan's room was just above his landlord's apartment. He had pulled up a piece of a floorboard. He could see and hear everything that went on below. The night after Bonacieux's arrest, he heard a woman's cries. And then muffled moans.

"The scoundrels!" muttered d'Artagnan. "They're tying her up and searching her!"

"But I tell you I live here!" cried the woman. "I'm Constance Bonacieux!"

"You're just the person we've been waiting for," said one of the men below.

"They've gagged her. Now they're

going to take her away!" cried d'Artagnan.

He sprang up and grabbed his sword.

"I'm going down to try to stop them."

"But, sir, you'll surely be killed!" said Planchet.

"Nonsense, you fool," snapped d'Artagnan.

He climbed out the window and hung from the sill. Then he dropped to the ground. He knocked on the front door and waited. The door opened. D'Artagnan rushed inside with his sword drawn.

A short time later, four of the cardinal's guards came running out the door. Their uniforms had been cut to ribbons.

D'Artagnan hurried over to Madame Bonacieux, who had fainted. He stood gazing at her. She was a lovely young woman with dark hair. For d'Artagnan, it was love at first sight.

Madame Bonacieux came to and looked around the room in terror. Then she saw that she was alone with her rescuer. She held out her hands to d'Artagnan.

"Thank you for saving me, sir," she said. "But how did you know I needed help?"

"Your husband told me you had been kidnapped. He asked me to rescue you. How did you escape?"

"I tied my sheets together and lowered myself out the window. I came home because I thought my husband was here. I need his help."

D'Artagnan told her what had happened to Monsieur Bonacieux. Then he said, "It is not safe for you to stay here, Madame. The guards will return soon."

"You're right," said Constance. "But I must go back to the palace. The queen needs me. Will you help me, Monsieur...?"

"D'Artagnan," said the young man, bowing. "And I am at your service, Madame. I knew from the first moment I saw you that I would do anything for you."

Constance's face turned pink. "Oh, thank you, Monsieur d'Artagnan," she whispered.

"Now, how can I help you?" he said.

"The cardinal's guards may be looking for me. Please follow me back to the palace to make sure I get there safely."

"No harm will come to you, my dear Constance," said d'Artagnan. "I swear it!"

They left the house very quietly and started down the street. D'Artagnan kept about twenty paces behind Constance. Then she stopped at a house and knocked three times at the door. It opened. A shadowy figure stepped outside and put his arm around Constance.

D'Artagnan was filled with a jealous rage. He rushed toward them, blocking their way.

"What do you want, sir?" asked the man, in a foreign accent. "Let us pass."

"Take your hands off this lady!" cried d'Artagnan, drawing his sword.

"In the name of heaven, Your Grace!" cried Constance. She stepped between the men and held back their swords.

"Your Grace!" exclaimed d'Artagnan.

"Yes," Constance whispered. "I am taking the Duke of Buckingham to the queen."

"Please forgive me, Your Grace," said d'Artagnan. "I love her, and I was jealous. You know what it is to be in love. Forgive me and tell me how I can serve you."

"You're a fine young man," said the duke. "You can serve us by following us to the palace. Kill anyone who tries to stop us!"

"I will, Your Grace!" said d'Artagnan.

He put his sword under his arm. Then he followed Constance and the duke to a side entrance of the palace. When they were safely inside, he headed for home.

CHAPTER 6

THE CARDINAL'S SPIES

Meanwhile, Monsieur Bonacieux had been arrested and taken to the Bastille. It was the most dreaded prison in France. One night he heard footsteps coming toward his cell. The door opened, and an officer stepped inside.

"Come with me," ordered the officer.

"Where are you taking me?" asked Bonacieux, terrified.

But the officer would not tell him. He led Bonacieux out of the Bastille and pushed him into a carriage. The carriage drove through Paris. It stopped at the back door of a house. The officer led Bonacieux down a hall, up a flight of stairs, and into a large study.

Standing in front of the fireplace was a gray-haired man. He had a proud face and piercing eyes. The man was Cardinal Richelieu.

"So you are Bonacieux," said the cardinal. "You are accused of plotting against France with your wife and the Duke of Buckingham."

"I know nothing about such a plot, Your Eminence," cried Bonacieux.

"You knew your wife had been kidnapped," said Richelieu. "Did you know that she has escaped?"

"Yes, they told me when I was in prison. But I don't know where she is. That's the truth. I swear it!" said Bonacieux.

The cardinal studied Bonacieux for a moment. Then he picked up a silver bell from the desk and rang it. Seconds later, a tall nobleman with dark hair and a scar on his forehead entered the room.

"That's him!" cried Bonacieux. "That's the man who kidnapped my wife!"

Richelieu rang the bell again. An officer stepped into the room. "Take this prisoner outside until I call for him," ordered the cardinal.

As soon as the door had closed behind Bonacieux, the cardinal spoke. "Well, Count Rochefort, what do you have to report?"

"The queen and the duke have seen each other at the palace," said Rochefort. "But there's more. One of the queen's ladies-in-waiting reported that she saw her majesty give Buckingham a box. Inside the box was a sash with twelve diamond studs on it. As you know, the king gave the queen those diamond studs on her last birthday."

"Good, very good," Richelieu said, smiling. "Now I shall write to Milady de Winter in London. I shall instruct her to steal two of the diamond studs and bring them to me. Those diamonds shall be the queen's downfall!"

He sat at his desk and quickly wrote the letter. After sealing it, he handed it to

Rochefort. "Give this letter to your fastest messenger," he told the count. "And send Bonacieux back in here."

Rochefort bowed deeply and left the room. A few moments later, Bonacieux entered.

"I am innocent, Your Eminence," cried the terrified man. He fell to his knees. "Please believe me!"

The cardinal held out his hand and said, "Stand up, my friend. You're a good man. I know that you have been unjustly arrested. Forgive me."

"The cardinal touched my hand!" Bonacieux said joyfully. "He called me his friend!"

"Here, my friend," said Richelieu. "Take this bag of three hundred pistoles."

"Oh, thank you, Your Eminence!"

"Good-bye, Monsieur Bonacieux, good-bye."

Bonacieux bowed low and backed out of the room. The cardinal's solemn expression turned into a wicked smile. "Now I have another spy," he said. "One who will spy on his wife."

A few weeks later, Richelieu received a letter from Milady. The letter said, "I have the two diamond studs. But I will need money to get back to Paris."

Richelieu figured out that it would take five days for the money to reach Milady. And it would take five days for Milady to travel from London to Paris.

He sent a messenger off to London with the money. Then he called on the king.

"Sire," he said. "The queen has seemed unhappy lately. Perhaps a ball would please her. And it would give her a chance to wear the twelve diamond studs you gave her on her birthday. She hasn't yet worn them."

"What a good idea!" said the king. "I shall inform her majesty at once. When shall we have the ball?"

"Ten days from now would be perfect, Sire," said the cardinal.

The king hurried to the queen's apart

ment. He told her the good news. That a ball would be held in her honor in ten days.

"And I shall expect you to wear the twelve diamond studs I gave you," the king added.

The queen turned pale. She curtsied and said in a low voice, "Yes, Sire."

After the king had left, she buried her face in her hands. She burst into tears.

"Is there anything I can do for you, Your Majesty?" asked a gentle voice.

The queen looked up and saw Constance Bonacieux standing in the doorway of a small dressing room.

"Oh, Constance, did you hear what the king said?" sobbed the queen. "What shall I do?"

Constance knelt down and took the queen's hands in hers. "You gave the twelve diamond studs to the Duke of Buckingham, didn't you?"

"Yes. And the cardinal must know that I do not have the studs. He plans to disgrace me at the ball."

"We must get the studs back from the duke," Constance said. "I will send my husband to London. I know I can trust him. But first you must write a letter to the duke. You must ask him to return the studs."

"Yes, yes," the queen said, hurrying to her desk. After she had written the letter, she sealed it. Then she went to her jewel case and took out a ring. "This ring is worth at least a thousand pistoles. Sell it and give the money to your husband for his journey."

"He'll leave within an hour, Your Majesty," Constance promised.

"If you succeed," the queen said softly, "you will have saved my honor and my life!"

Constance put the letter and the ring in her pocket and hurried away.

Minutes later she rushed through the door of her house. "We must talk," she said to her husband. "You can do a good deed and make a lot of money at the same time."

Bonacieux looked at his wife with interest. "How much money?" he asked.

"A thousand pistoles," Constance said. "You must deliver this letter to a very important person in London."

"More plots? No, thank you! I know better than to get mixed up in any more plots. The cardinal has opened my eyes."

"The cardinal!" exclaimed Constance. "You've seen the cardinal?"

"Yes! He called me his friend and gave me this bag filled with three hundred pistoles," said Bonacieux. "I won't allow you to plot against him and France for the sake of the queen!"

"So you are working for the cardinal now. Is that it?" Constance said. Her eyes blazed with anger. "You're nothing but a greedy, cowardly traitor!"

Bonacieux suddenly decided to learn more about this trip. It might interest the cardinal. So he smiled sweetly at his wife.

"My dear Constance," he said. "Don't be angry with me. I will do as you ask. Just tell me whom I must deliver this letter to in London."

But by now, Constance knew better than to trust her husband. "Never mind," she said. "The letter isn't important. It's just a list of trinkets to buy in London."

Bonacieux was sure she was lying. He decided to go to the cardinal and tell him that the queen was sending a letter to London.

"I'm afraid I must leave for an appointment," he said. "But I'll come back soon."

"You villain!" Constance said as soon as he had left. "I never loved you, Monsieur Bonacieux. And now I hate you! I shall make you pay for your treachery!"

Just then, a tapping sound above her made her raise her head. A voice called through a hole in the ceiling.

"Constance! Open the back door. I'm coming down to see you."

CHAPTER 7

JOURNEY TO LONDON

Constance opened the door. D'Artagnan stepped into the apartment.

"You heard?" asked Constance.

"Every word," d'Artagnan said. "The queen needs a brave, intelligent, and loyal man to go to London for her. Here I am!"

Constance smiled at him. "Thank you, d'Artagnan. I know I can trust you."

"I could never betray you or the queen. I would rather die!"

Constance opened a cupboard. She took out the bag of pistoles her husband had shown her.

"Here," she said. "Take this money. You will need it for your journey."

D'Artagnan burst out laughing. "The

cardinal's money!" he exclaimed. "I shall save the queen with His Eminence's money. That's very funny!"

"Dear d'Artagnan," said Constance. "Now I must get back to the queen. And you must start for London!"

D'Artagnan left and hurried to Monsieur de Tréville's house. He told Tréville that he had to travel to London. It was a secret mission for the queen.

"The cardinal's guards will try to stop you," warned Tréville. "You need four men for such a mission. That way, at least one man is sure to get through."

"You're right, sir. I would like to take Athos, Porthos, and Aramis with me."

"I will arrange it," said Tréville. "And you will need passes releasing you from your regiment." He gave d'Artagnan four passes and wished him luck.

An hour later the four friends galloped out of Paris. They rode north toward the port of Calais. The journey went well until they stopped at an inn for breakfast.

They had finished their meal and were getting ready to leave. Just then, a man at the next table asked Porthos to drink a toast to the cardinal.

"Certainly," said Porthos. "Will you also drink to the king?"

"I will never drink to the king," cried the man. He drew his sword.

The others knew Porthos would never walk away from a fight. So they had no choice but to leave the inn without him.

Two hours later the three riders came upon some men working on the road. Suddenly, the workmen grabbed muskets from a ditch. They began firing.

"It's an ambush!" shouted d'Artagnan. "Don't shoot back! Keep riding!"

A bullet struck Aramis in the shoulder. He continued riding. But after a few hours he was too weak to go on. Athos and d'Artagnan took him to an inn to recover. Then they rode on alone.

At midnight, they stopped at an inn for the night. The next morning, Athos went to pay the bill. The innkeeper looked at the coins.

"This is counterfeit money," said the innkeeper. "I'm going to have you and your friend arrested!"

"You lying scoundrel!" roared Athos. "I'll cut off your ears!"

Suddenly, four armed men came into the room and rushed at him.

"I'm trapped!" Athos shouted. "Go, d'Artagnan! Hurry!"

D'Artagnan didn't wait to be told again. He jumped on his horse and galloped away.

Later that day he reached Calais. As he neared the dock, he recognized the tall, dark-haired man talking to the ship's captain. He hid behind a barrel and listened.

"I can't take you on my ship unless you have a pass from the cardinal," d'Artagnan heard the captain say.

"I have that pass here," the man said. He took out a paper from his pocket.

The captain looked at the pass and

returned it. "That's fine, Count Rochefort," he said. "We sail in an hour."

Rochefort nodded and left the dock. D'Artagnan followed him to a small wooded area. Then d'Artagnan called out, "Count Rochefort!"

The count turned. "Well, if it isn't my young Gascon hothead from Meung!"

D'Artagnan drew his sword. "Give me that pass!" he cried.

"If you want it, you'll have to take it!" snarled Rochefort. He drew his sword.

The two men lunged at each other. In three minutes, d'Artagnan wounded Rochefort three times. With each sword thrust, d'Artagnan cried, "One for Athos! One for Porthos! One for Aramis!"

At the third thrust, Rochefort fell. Thinking he was dead or unconscious, d'Artagnan bent down to take the pass. Suddenly, Rochefort plunged his sword into d'Artagnan's chest, crying, "One for you!"

"And one for me!" shouted d'Artagnan, thrusting his sword into Rochefort.

He found the pass and hurried to the ship. On board, he examined his wound. It was not serious. But he was very tired from his long journey. He stretched out on the deck and went to sleep.

The next morning, the ship docked at the port of Dover, and d'Artagnan stepped onto English soil. He hired a horse and galloped off toward London.

CHAPTER 8

THE DIAMOND STUDS

Four hours later d'Artagnan arrived at the Duke of Buckingham's mansion in London. The duke's personal servant answered the door.

"I have come from Paris on a matter of life and death," d'Artagnan told the man. "I must speak with your master at once!"

"How shall I announce you to His Grace?" asked the servant.

"Just tell him I'm the young man who challenged him to a duel in Paris."

Buckingham came to the door immediately. "Has anything happened to the queen?" he asked anxiously.

"No, Your Grace. But she is in grave danger. This letter will explain everything."

"Oh, my poor Anne!" exclaimed the duke when he had read the letter. "Come with me, d'Artagnan. Quickly!"

He led d'Artagnan through the house to a large bedroom. He hurried to a door hidden in the wall. He unlocked it with a small gold key that was hanging from his neck. Then he led d'Artagnan into a small chapel lit up by dozens of candles. A portrait of Queen Anne hung on the wall above an altar.

The duke stepped over to the altar and opened a box. "Here are the precious diamond studs," he said. He lifted a sash from the box and cried out in alarm.

"What's wrong, Your Grace?" asked d'Artagnan.

"There are only ten studs here!" he exclaimed. "Two studs are missing!"

"Could you have lost them?"

"No, they were stolen. But who... Ah, I remember! The only time I've worn them was at court last week. I spent most of the evening with Milady de Winter. She must have stolen them for the cardinal."

"Milady and the diamond studs are probably on their way to Paris by now," said d'Artagnan.

"Tell me, when is the king's ball to take place?" asked Buckingham.

"Next Monday."

"Then we still have five days," said the duke. He left the chapel, carrying the diamond-studded sash. D'Artagnan followed, wondering what the duke was going to do.

Buckingham sent his servant to find his jeweler. When the jeweler arrived, the duke said, "Look at these diamonds. Tell me how much each one is worth."

The jeweler examined the diamonds carefully. Then he said, "One thousand pounds each, Your Grace."

"And how long would it take you to make two more diamond studs? As you can see, two are missing."

"At least a week, Your Grace."

"I'll need the two studs by tomorrow night," said Buckingham. "I'll give you four thousand pounds if you can do it."

"You shall have them, Your Grace," the jeweler said, bowing.

The next day, the jeweler delivered the two new diamond studs as he had promised. They were perfect copies.

"Here," Buckingham said, handing the sash to d'Artagnan. "I have done all I can. Take this sash to the queen with my love."

"Right away, Your Grace," promised d'Artagnan.

"I have a ship waiting to take you to France. There will be horses for you when you arrive. And now, young man, give me your hand. We may meet on the battlefield soon. But today we part as friends."

D'Artagnan shook the duke's hand. Then he bowed and left the house.

His journey to Paris went smoothly. He reached the city on the evening of the ball. He stopped first at Monsieur de Tréville's house for news of the three musketeers.

"They have returned and are recovering from their wounds," Tréville told him.

Next, d'Artagnan went to the palace to deliver the diamond-studded sash to the queen.

Then he joined his regiment, which was on duty at the palace.

Meanwhile, the guests were gathering in the ballroom. They bowed deeply as the queen entered. At the same moment, the cardinal and the king came in. There was a sinister smile on Richelieu's face. He looked at the queen. She was not wearing her diamond-studded sash.

Richelieu whispered something to the king. Louis went up to the queen and said, "Madame, will you tell me why you're not wearing your diamond studs? You knew I wanted to see them."

"Sire, I was afraid I might lose them in this great crowd." The queen spoke in a trembling voice.

"You were wrong not to do as I asked, Madame!" the king said angrily.

"I can go to my room and put them on, Sire," said the queen.

"Do so at once, Madame! The ball is about to begin."

As soon as she had left, the cardinal handed the king a box. The king opened it and saw two diamond studs.

"What is the meaning of this?" he asked.

"I doubt that the queen will wear her diamond studs," said the cardinal. "If she does, count them, Sire. If there are only ten, ask her what happened to the other two."

Just then, a cry of admiration rose up from the crowd. Everyone gazed at the beautiful queen of France, who was entering the ballroom. Pinned from her shoulder to her waist was the diamond-studded sash.

"Madame," said the king, "I thank you for obeying my wishes. But I believe two of your diamond studs are missing. I've brought them to you."

He held out the two studs the cardinal had given him.

The queen pretended to be surprised. "You're giving me two more, Sire?" she said. "Now I have fourteen."

The king counted the diamond studs on her sash. There were twelve.

He turned to the cardinal. "What does this mean?" he asked sternly.

"It means, Sire, that I wanted to give those two studs to Her Majesty. But I did not dare to do it myself. So I chose to give them to her through you."

The queen's smile showed that she was not fooled by Richelieu's lie. "I'm very grateful to you, Your Eminence," she said sweetly. "I'm sure that those two studs cost you as much as the other twelve cost His Majesty."

She bowed to the king and slowly made her way through the ballroom. She stopped in front of d'Artagnan. He was on guard in the ballroom. She smiled and held out her hand. D'Artagnan knelt down, took her hand, and kissed it. He felt an object pressed into his hand. The queen had given him a ring to thank him.

Two of the guests watched them with

interest—Cardinal Richelieu and Milady de Winter.

"So d'Artagnan and that Bonacieux woman have outwitted you," Milady said. "What will you do to them?"

"Rochefort will deal with Madame Bonacieux," said the cardinal. "He has nearly recovered from the wounds that young Gascon gave him. I could use a brave man like d'Artagnan on my side. Perhaps I will try to win his friendship."

Milady snapped her fan shut. "Because of him, I failed in my mission. I do not like to fail. D'Artagnan shall pay dearly for what he has done. I swear it!"

CHAPTER 9

ATHOS' SECRET

D'Artagnan was placed on guard duty at the palace for the next few days. One day, as he was on his way home, he spotted a carriage. A man was trying to pull a beautiful blond young woman out the window.

D'Artagnan drew his sword and rushed toward the carriage, shouting, "You there! Take your hands off that woman!"

The woman glanced at d'Artagnan. Then she whispered to her attacker, "Go, quickly! You've played your part well."

The man ran off and disappeared down a side street. D'Artagnan hurried over to the carriage.

"Are you hurt, Madame?" he asked, recognizing her as Milady de Winter.

"Oh, no, Monsieur," said Milady. "Thank you for coming to my rescue. How can I reward you?"

"I am rewarded by seeing that you are safe," d'Artagnan said with a bow.

"You are a very gallant young man," Milady said, smiling. "I would be pleased if you would call on me later. Here is my name and address."

"I will be honored, Madame," said d'Artagnan.

The coachman cracked his whip, and the carriage drove off. D'Artagnan continued on to Athos' house, where he was staying.

He told Athos what had just happened.

"Beware of her, my friend," said Athos. "Didn't you tell me that she is one of the cardinal's spies?"

"Yes," d'Artagnan replied. "Perhaps I can learn something from her about his plans. Besides, she is very beautiful."

"Never trust a woman like that, beautiful or not." Athos looked at d'Artagnan for a moment. Then he said, "Let me tell you what a beautiful woman did to a friend of mine.

"This man was the Count de la Fère. He was a rich, young nobleman who could have married any woman he chose. But he fell in love with a young woman who was beautiful and poor. She had just come to live in his province. He knew nothing about her.

"La Fère gave her his name, his wealth, and his love. But he was a fool!"

"Why, if he loved her?" asked d'Artagnan.

"One day he found out a terrible secret about her. They were out riding. She fell from her horse, and her dress slipped down over her shoulder. There, burned into her bare shoulder, was a lily. She had been branded as a criminal by the public executioner!"

"What did the count do?" d'Artagnan asked.

"The law allowed him to put her to death. So he hanged her from a tree."

Athos buried his face in his hands. Then

he raised his head and stared straight ahead. "And that cured me of trusting beautiful women," he muttered.

D'Artagnan had suspected that the count in the story was Athos himself. Now he was sure.

"I am sorry for you, my friend," he said gently. "But I do not believe that I have anything to fear from Milady. I'm going to call on her now."

Milady's maid opened the door. "Please wait in the hall, sir," she said. "I'll see if my mistress is at home."

Soon d'Artagnan could hear voices coming from another room. He listened at the door.

"But how can you make him love you?" the maid asked Milady. "I have heard that he is in love with someone else."

"Oh, that Bonacieux woman," Milady said scornfully. "Count Rochefort and I have taken care of her. D'Artagnan will soon forget all about her. I will make him fall in love with me. Then I will kill him!"

D'Artagnan did not wait to hear more. He burst into the room crying, "You miserable woman! What have you done to Constance Bonacieux?"

Milady turned pale and backed away from d'Artagnan. She opened a drawer, pulled out a small dagger, and sprang at him. D'Artagnan grabbed her wrist and twisted the knife from her hand.

"Where is Constance?" he cried, tightening his hold on her wrist. "Tell me or I'll kill you!"

With her other hand, Milady pulled a large brooch off her dress. She aimed the pin of the brooch at d'Artagnan's eye.

D'Artagnan grabbed the brooch out of her hand. As he did, he loosened his grip on her wrist. She broke free. Then she rushed to a table and picked up another dagger.

As she came at him, he drew his sword. The point of the sword caught on the sleeve of her dress. The top part of the sleeve ripped in two.

D'Artagnan gasped in horror. On Milady's bare shoulder was a small red lily. It was the brand of the public executioner.

"Villain!" she shrieked. "You've discovered my secret! Now you will die!"

She lunged at him with her dagger. D'Artagnan jumped back just as she thrust the dagger at his heart. He turned and raced out of the house into the street. He didn't stop running until he reached Athos' house.

"What's happened, my boy?" asked Athos as d'Artagnan burst in upon him.

D'Artagnan sat on the nearest chair to catch his breath. He was still clutching Milady's brooch. He opened his fingers and looked at it. Raising his head, he saw that Athos was staring down at the brooch.

"Have you seen this brooch before?" d'Artagnan asked.

"It looks like one that used to belong to my family," Athos said. He took it out of d'Artagnan's hand and examined it.

"Do you recognize it?" asked d'Artagnan.

"Yes. It's the same brooch. I gave it to that woman...my wife. But how did you get it?"

D'Artagnan told him everything that had taken place at Milady's house. When he mentioned the brand on her shoulder, Athos turned pale.

"This woman you call Milady," said Athos. "Is she blond?"

"Yes," replied d'Artagnan.

"Does she have light-blue eyes and black eyebrows and eyelashes?"

"Yes."

"Is she tall?"

"Yes."

"And the lily on her shoulder. Is it small and red?"

D'Artagnan nodded. Then he said, "Milady is your wife. Isn't she?"

"Yes," Athos whispered. "I had hoped that she was dead."

"You must be careful, Athos," said d'Artagnan. "You tried to kill her once. She may try to kill you for revenge."

"She won't come after me. She thinks the Count de la Fère is dead. She doesn't know that he has become the musketeer Athos. But now that you know her secret, she will stop at nothing to find you and kill you."

"My regiment leaves for La Rochelle tomorrow," said d'Artagnan. "I'll be far away from her."

"Be warned, my boy. You can never be far enough away from that evil woman!"

CHAPTER 10

A MEETING AT THE RED DOVE INN

The next adventure of d'Artagnan and the three musketeers began in the seaport of La Rochelle.

The citizens of La Rochelle were French Protestants, called Huguenots. Cardinal Richelieu had ordered them to become Catholics. But the Huguenots decided to fight rather than give up their religion. The cardinal and the king arrived in La Rochelle to force the rebels to surrender. Athos, Porthos, Aramis, and d'Artagnan were among the troops.

One evening d'Artagnan and the three musketeers met at the inn where d'Artagnan was staying.

"Thank you for sending this wine," said

d'Artagnan. He uncorked a bottle and filled four glasses. "Let's drink a toast to friendship."

"We didn't send you any wine," said Athos quietly.

Porthos raised his glass. "Who cares?" he said. "Let's drink it anyway." He put the glass to his lips.

Aramis snatched the glass away before Porthos could drink from it. "None of us should drink the wine until we find out where it came from," Aramis said firmly.

"But if you didn't send it, then who..." d'Artagnan began. Suddenly, he remembered something and turned pale. "Come with me, quickly!" he cried.

He rushed out of the inn, followed by his friends. The first thing they saw was a soldier lying dead on the ground. An empty wineglass lay on the ground next to him.

"I gave him a glass of that wine," d'Artagnan said in a trembling voice. "I swear I didn't know..."

"...that it was poisoned," Athos finished. "We can all guess who sent it."

"Milady!" d'Artagnan said with a shudder. "You were right, Athos. She is a monster who will stop at nothing to get revenge!"

"She will surely try to kill you again," Athos said. "But how? And when?"

A few nights later, the three musketeers spent the evening at the Red Dove Inn. D'Artagnan's regiment was on duty, so he wasn't able to join them.

Athos, Porthos, and Aramis were on their way back to camp. They saw two riders coming toward them.

"Who goes there?" called Athos. His hand was on his pistol.

"Who are you?" one of the strangers said in a deep, clear voice.

"It must be an officer making his night rounds," Athos said to his friends.

"Answer me or you'll regret it," called the same voice.

"We're the king's musketeers," Athos replied.

The riders came closer. Long cloaks hid their faces. The man who had spoken before said, "Your names, gentlemen."

"What right do you have to question us?" Athos demanded.

The stranger let the cloak fall away from his face.

"The cardinal!" Athos cried out.

"Your name?" the cardinal asked again.

"Athos, Your Eminence."

"Ah, yes," said the cardinal. "And the two men with you must be Monsieur Porthos and Monsieur Aramis. I know that you are not exactly my friends. But I also know that you are brave men who can be trusted. So I shall ask you to accompany me to the Red Dove Inn. I shall feel safer with three musketeers at my side."

"We will be honored, Your Eminence," said Athos.

When they arrived at the inn, the cardinal told his guard to wait outside. Then he asked the innkeeper, "Do you have a room where these musketeers can warm themselves while they wait for me?"

The innkeeper led Athos, Porthos, and Aramis to a large room on the ground floor. The cardinal hurried up the stairs.

Porthos and Aramis sat by the fire playing a game of dice. Athos paced back and forth. He was wondering whom the cardinal was meeting in such secrecy.

Athos passed in front of a broken stovepipe. The stovepipe ran up through the ceiling into the room above.

Suddenly, Athos heard the murmur of voices coming from the stovepipe. He signaled to his friends to be quiet. He kept his ear close to the open end of the pipe. The cardinal was talking.

"Listen, Milady. Here are your orders."

"Milady!" murmured Athos.

"You are to leave for England tonight to meet with the Duke of Buckingham," said the cardinal.

Athos told his friends to bolt the door and then come and listen with him.

"But I fear the duke will not trust me.

Not after the theft of the diamond studs," said a woman's voice.

"You won't need to gain his trust," said the cardinal. "You will simply deliver a message. Tell him that if he sends English troops to help the Huguenots, it will mean ruin for the queen. And disgrace for him in England."

"What if he doesn't believe me?"

"Just tell him I have the proof that will destroy them both."

"And if the duke refuses to cancel his plans?" asked Milady.

"Then he must be killed," the cardinal said calmly. Athos gasped.

"I will see to it, Your Eminence," said Milady. "And then I will take care of *my* enemies. First, that Bonacieux woman."

"But she is in prison," said the cardinal.

"Not any longer. The queen found out where she was and had her taken to a convent for safety. I would like to know the name of that convent."

"I shall find out and let you know," said Richelieu.

"Good," said Milady. "And now, let me tell you about a man who is your enemy as well as mine. I'm speaking of d'Artagnan."

"I can easily send him to the Bastille for the rest of his life."

"The life of d'Artagnan for the life of Buckingham," Milady said. "That's a fair trade! Now, I will need a letter from you. It should allow me to do anything I need to for the good of France."

A moment later Athos heard the scratching sounds of pen on paper. He led Porthos and Aramis away from the stovepipe.

"I must leave you now," he said softly.

"But what shall we tell the cardinal?" asked Porthos.

"Tell him I've gone on ahead to make sure the road is safe."

"Be careful, Athos!" said Aramis.

"I will, my friend. Don't worry," Athos

said as he rushed out of the room.

He got on his horse and galloped away. When he was out of sight of the inn, he stopped behind some bushes. He waited until he saw his friends and the cardinal pass by. Then he rode back to the inn.

"My officer asked me to deliver a message. It's for the lady on the second floor," he told the innkeeper.

"Go up to her room," said the innkeeper. "She's still there."

Athos quietly climbed the stairs. Through the open door of her room, he saw Milady putting on her hat.

Athos slipped into the room, closed the door, and bolted it. Milady turned when she heard the sound of the lock.

"Who are you?" she cried. "What do you want?"

Athos took off his hat and cloak and walked toward her. "Do you recognize me, Madame?"

"The Count de la Fère!" she gasped. She turned pale and backed away from him.

"Yes, Madame. You thought I was dead, just as I thought you were dead. The Count de la Fère has been hidden behind the name of the musketeer Athos. And the criminal Anne de Breuil has been hidden behind the name Milady de Winter!"

"What do you want with me?" Milady whispered.

"Listen to me carefully, Madame," Athos said coldly. "I don't care what you do to the Duke of Buckingham. He is an Englishman and my enemy. But d'Artagnan is my loyal friend. If you touch one hair on his head, I swear I will kill you."

"He is my enemy," Milady said. "And he must die."

Athos drew his pistol. "Give me the letter the cardinal wrote for you."

Milady did not move. Athos aimed his pistol at her head. "You have one second to hand over the letter," he said calmly.

Milady quickly reached into her pocket and pulled out the letter. "Take it!" she cried, handing it to him.

Athos unfolded the paper and read, "The bearer of this letter has acted under my orders and for the good of France." The letter was signed, "Richelieu."

Athos put on his hat and cloak. "I wish you good night, Madame. Now that I've taken away your permission to murder d'Artagnan."

And he left the room without looking back.

He rode to the inn where d'Artagnan was staying. The young man had just come off duty. He was sitting by the fire with Porthos and Aramis. They both had arrived a few moments earlier.

The three musketeers told d'Artagnan what they had overheard at the Red Dove Inn.

"We must warn the queen," said d'Artagnan. "And she must warn the duke."

"We can't leave our posts in the middle of battle," Athos said. "Especially not to save an enemy of France like Buckingham. We'd be guilty of treason!"

"That's true," said d'Artagnan. He suddenly had an idea. "But we can send my trusted Planchet!"

He wrote a letter and sealed it. Then he called his servant over to him. "You must ride to Paris at once. Deliver this letter to the queen," he told Planchet. "Then carry the queen's message to the Duke of Buckingham in London."

"I'll ride like the wind, sir," Planchet promised. He put on his hat, took the letter, and rushed out the door.

"Let us hope he arrives in time to keep Milady from carrying out her murderous plans," said d'Artagnan.

CHAPTER 11

MILADY'S EVIL PLAN

Milady's journey to England took longer than usual because of bad weather. Finally, her ship docked at Portsmouth. On the same day, Planchet arrived in the town to wait for a ship to take him back to France.

As she stepped off the ship, Milady saw the Duke of Buckingham on the pier. She started toward him. But a young officer and several guards blocked her way.

"Please come with us, Madame," the officer said quietly.

"But I have an important message for the duke," Milady insisted. "It comes from Cardinal Richelieu himself!"

"I'm sorry, Madame. You may not see

the duke. Now, please come with us."

Milady looked down at the pistols in their hands and knew she had no choice.

The officer led her to a carriage. The carriage drove swiftly out of the city.

"At least tell me where you are taking me!" Milady cried.

The officer did not reply. He seemed to have turned into a statue.

Milady tried to open the door.

"Be careful," the officer said calmly. "If you jump out, you'll be killed."

Milady sat back in her seat. She tried to think of ways to escape, but nothing came to mind.

The carriage stopped at a castle on the edge of a steep cliff. Milady was taken to a room. The door and window had bars on them.

"Am I a prisoner then?" Milady asked, turning pale. "What crime have I committed? What will happen to me?"

"My orders were to bring you here and guard you," said the officer. "My name is

John Felton. I am a lieutenant in the duke's personal guards. I do not know what the duke's plans are for you. But while you are here, you will be treated well."

He turned and left the room, bolting the door behind him.

Milady stared at the door, her face twisted with rage. She almost screamed at Felton, but she stopped herself.

"I must remain calm," she murmured. "I will need all my energy and wits to think of a way to escape from this place."

She sank into an armchair and sat for hours, lost in thought.

When Felton brought in her supper, she was kneeling by the chair, praying out loud. Felton was a Protestant and a very religious man. He knew the prayers she was saying. He watched her for a moment. Then he put the tray down and left. As soon as the door closed, he heard Milady sobbing. When he came to take the tray away later, he saw that she had eaten very little.

This went on for several days. Felton

began to feel pity for the beautiful young woman. And soon that pity turned to love.

On the fifth day, Felton brought a tray into Milady's room as usual. "You must eat, Madame," he said gently. "I cannot bear to see you become ill."

Milady stopped praying and raised her tear-stained face. "Please let me die," she begged. "Or better still, give me a knife so that I can end my life quickly. Then I will be free forever from the man who has betrayed both me and his country!"

"What man?" Felton asked. "Tell me!"

"It's the man who swore to marry me. Then he broke his promise. I was too poor to be a duke's wife," Milady sobbed. "It's the man who loves the queen of France so much he will betray his country for her!"

"Buckingham!" cried Felton angrily. "It's the Duke of Buckingham!"

Milady buried her face in her hands and nodded. Felton knelt down beside her and took her in his arms.

"I will not let you die," he said softly. "I

can't bear this! I will help you to escape."

He stood up and left the room. Milady smiled. Her plan had worked!

A few hours later she heard a tapping sound at her window. She ran to the window and opened it.

"Felton!" she cried. "I knew you would come back to save me!"

"Yes, but we must hurry," said Felton. "I'm going to saw through the bars. Then I'll carry you down the ladder. Wait until you hear my signal."

Milady lay down on the bed and waited. She could hear the wind moaning and the sound of rain beating against the walls.

Finally, she heard Felton tap against the windowpane. She hurried over to the window and climbed out of the opening he had made. She put her arms around his neck. Slowly and carefully, Milady and Felton made their way down the cliff.

When they reached the ground, Felton led Milady to a small boat. They climbed in, and Felton picked up the oars.

"I have hired a ship to take you back to France," he said. "I'm taking you there now."

"Thank you, Felton. Thank you!" said Milady. "But what about Buckingham? He must pay for his evil deeds!"

"Don't worry, my love. I will take care of him when you are safely on the ship."

Milady looked at the young man beside her and smiled. The death of the duke was written all over his face.

Felton helped Milady aboard the ship. "I will be back here at ten o'clock," he told her. "Then we will travel to France together."

"I will wait for you, my love," Milady said sweetly.

Felton kissed her hand. He got back into his boat and rowed toward Portsmouth.

When he reached the pier, he walked to the house where the duke was staying. His hand clutched a knife hidden in his doublet.

Buckingham was coming out of the house. He frowned when he saw Felton.

"You are supposed to be guarding that woman," the duke snapped. "What are you doing here?"

Felton plunged the knife into Buckingham's heart. "Milady has been avenged!" he cried. The duke fell to the ground, dead.

A plump, young Frenchman watched the scene with horror. It was Planchet, d'Artagnan's servant. Now he would have one more message to deliver. He would have to tell his master and his friends about the murder of the Duke of Buckingham.

Meanwhile, Felton had been surrounded by guards. As they were dragging him away, he heard a clock strike nine. He looked out over the harbor. Milady's ship was sailing for the coast of France. Milady had not waited for him, as she had promised.

Felton realized that he had been tricked. But it was too late. He had helped the woman he loved carry out her evil plan. Now he would pay with his life.

CHAPTER 12

A TERRIBLE MURDER

When Milady reached France, she wrote to Cardinal Richelieu: "You may be sure that the Duke of Buckingham will not leave for France. Milady."

The next day a carriage drove up to the inn where Milady had spent the night. Count Rochefort got out. He was shown up to her room.

"His Eminence received your letter a few hours ago," said Rochefort. "He was very pleased with your success."

"Good," said Milady. "Now I can take care of my own business. Has His Eminence learned where Constance Bonacieux is hidden?"

"The cardinal *always* finds out what he

wishes to know. Madame Bonacieux is at the convent in Bethune."

"Then I must leave for Bethune at once."

They went down the stairs. As they walked toward the carriage, they passed Planchet. He had just arrived from England. Neither Rochefort nor Milady recognized d'Artagnan's servant.

The count untied a horse from the back of the carriage. "I must return to the cardinal at La Rochelle," Rochefort said as he swung into the saddle.

"Give my regards to His Eminence," said Milady, stepping into the carriage.

"Give mine to the devil, Milady," said Rochefort.

They smiled at each other. Then Rochefort galloped off.

"Milady," muttered Planchet. "Isn't that the name of the woman who tried to kill my master?"

Then he heard Milady order the coachman to drive to the convent at Bethune.

"Bethune!" exclaimed Planchet. "That's where the queen said Madame Bonacieux is hiding. I must warn my master."

He hired a horse and galloped toward La Rochelle. Two hours later, he burst into d'Artagnan's room.

"Welcome back, Planchet!" said d'Artagnan. "You've come at a great moment. La Rochelle has surrendered at last! But what news do you bring?"

"Oh, sir, I have terrible news," Planchet said breathlessly. "The duke has been murdered. I was there, and I saw everything. The man who did it shouted out Milady's name."

"So once again that evil woman has outwitted us," d'Artagnan said bitterly. Then he asked, "Did you find out where Constance is?"

Planchet told him, adding, "But I overheard Milady tell her coachman to drive there."

"Oh, no!" cried d'Artagnan. "I must reach Constance before she does. Quickly,

Planchet, find Athos, Porthos, and Aramis. Bring them to me. We must ride to Bethune as fast as we can!"

Soon the four friends were galloping away toward Bethune.

Meanwhile, Milady's carriage had arrived at the convent. She asked to see the Mother Superior.

"I am here on the orders of His Eminence, the cardinal," Milady told the Mother Superior. "I have brought a message from him for Madame Bonacieux."

"Come in, my child," said the Mother Superior. "You will find Constance in her room. It is at the top of the stairs."

Milady climbed the stairs and knocked on the door. "Come in," a sweet voice called out.

Milady stepped into the room. She smiled at the young woman sitting in a chair by the window.

"Madame Bonacieux?" said Milady. "I am here to bring you some good news."

Constance stood up to meet the

stranger. "Who are you, Madame?" she asked.

"I am a friend of the man who loves you. I'm speaking of d'Artagnan, of course. He is on his way here for you now."

"D'Artagnan, coming for me? Oh, that is wonderful news!" said Constance.

"He asked me to stay with you until he arrives. But it will take him a few hours to reach Bethune. That will give us time to have dinner."

A short time later, their dinner was brought into the room. Milady put some chicken on a plate and gave it to Constance. But the young woman could only eat a few mouthfuls.

"Come, come, my dear child," said Milady. "You must eat more than that! You will need your strength for the long ride back to Paris."

"Forgive me, Madame," Constance said softly. "I am much too excited to eat."

"Well, at least have a glass of wine," urged Milady. She turned and poured wine into two glasses. She opened a large ring on her finger. Reddish powder slipped into one of the glasses. She handed that glass to Constance.

Milady raised her glass to her lips. "Now, let us drink to love!" she said.

As Constance drank up her glass of wine, the two women heard the sounds of horses.

Milady hurried to the window and recognized d'Artagnan and the three musketeers. She turned and ran out of the room.

"Wait for me," gasped Constance. She took two steps, then sank to the floor.

D'Artagnan and his friends rushed into the room. D'Artagnan knelt down and took Constance in his arms. She opened her eyes and gazed at him.

"Oh, d'Artagnan, my love," she whispered. "You've come for me at last." Then her eyes closed, and she went limp.

"She's fainted!" cried d'Artagnan.

Porthos shouted for help. Aramis ran to pour out a glass of water for her. But he stopped short. He saw Athos staring in horror at an empty wine glass in his hand.

D'Artagnan realized that Constance had been poisoned. Yet he still clung to her lifeless body.

Athos slowly walked over to d'Artagnan and put his arms around him. D'Artagnan burst into sobs.

"We will avenge her, my friend," Athos said quietly. "But now you must let her go. We must leave her with these good nuns."

D'Artagnan wiped the tears from his cheeks. He stood up and followed his friends out of the room. On the way down the stairs, he stopped to pick up a piece of paper. One sentence was written on it. He showed the paper to Athos, who nodded.

"I know that handwriting. It's Milady's. So she is waiting for Rochefort at the inn in Armentières. Well, she will soon be seeing us instead!"

CHAPTER 13

THE MAN IN THE RED CLOAK

D'Artagnan and the three musketeers galloped at top speed toward Armentières. When they reached the inn, they saw Milady sitting alone in a room on the ground floor.

They entered the room and shut the door. Milady screamed when she saw them. Athos quickly tied her hands behind her back.

"Guard her well, my friends. She must not escape this time. I'll be back in an hour."

He handed d'Artagnan the letter he had taken from Milady in La Rochelle. "If anyone asks any questions, show them this letter from the cardinal."

He rode off. An hour later, he returned. With him was a tall man in a red cloak. His face was covered by a black mask.

"Madame," said Athos. "We are now going to judge your crimes. D'Artagnan, you will be the first accuser."

D'Artagnan stepped forward. "I accuse this woman of poisoning Constance Bonacieux. I accuse her of trying to poison me with wine sent in the name of my friends. A brave soldier died in my place. Finally, I accuse her of arranging the murder of the Duke of Buckingham."

"Now it's my turn," said Athos. "I married this woman against the wishes of my family. I gave her my love and my wealth. Then I discovered that she was branded."

"You cannot prove the crime for which I was branded!" cried Milady. "You cannot find the man who branded me!"

"I will answer that," said the man in the red cloak. He took off his mask.

"It's the executioner of Lille!" shrieked Milady. "The man who branded me!"

"Hear my story," said the man. "This woman forced my brother to help her steal sacred treasures from the church. They were caught. But the woman escaped. My brother was sentenced to be branded and to serve ten years in jail. As the public executioner, I had to brand my own brother!

"I tracked the woman down and branded her as the thief she was. Then my brother escaped. Everyone thought I had helped him. I was thrown in jail in his place. He found out and gave himself up. That very night, he hanged himself in his cell. Now you know the crimes I accuse her of and why I branded her."

"Gentlemen," said Athos. "You have heard her crimes. What is your sentence?"

"Death!" said Porthos.

"Death!" said Aramis.

"Death!" said d'Artagnan.

"Death!" said the executioner of Lille.

"And I say death!" said Athos.

Milady let out a desperate scream. Then the strong hand of the executioner led her down to the river. The four friends followed. The executioner carried her to a small boat.

"Cowards! Murderers!" she shrieked.

When the boat reached the opposite shore, the executioner led her onto land. "Die in peace," he said. He raised his sword. There was a terrible cry and then the thud of Milady's headless body.

The executioner spread his red cloak on the ground and placed the dead woman on it. He tied the cloak together and carried the body back to the boat.

He rowed to the middle of the river and stopped. Then he dropped the body into the river. The water closed over it.

"Justice has been done," said Athos.

CHAPTER 14

THE FOUR MUSKETEERS

D'Artagnan and the three musketeers returned to La Rochelle. One evening they were sitting in a tavern when Count Rochefort stepped inside.

"You!" said d'Artagnan, jumping to his feet. "You won't escape me this time!"

"I don't need to escape from you," said Rochefort. "Because this time I'm looking for you. Monsieur d'Artagnan, I arrest you in the name of the cardinal. My orders are to bring you to His Eminence at once."

"Do not fear, my friend," said Athos. "We'll go with you."

Rochefort led them to the house where Richelieu was staying. They waited for the cardinal to return.

When the cardinal arrived, he motioned for d'Artagnan to follow him inside.

"We'll be waiting for you, d'Artagnan," said Athos. He wanted the cardinal to hear.

The cardinal and d'Artagnan went into the study. Richelieu stood behind a long table and looked at the young man.

"Monsieur," said the cardinal. "You are a traitor to France."

D'Artagnan knew this was the work of Milady. "And who has accused me of treason, Your Eminence? A woman who was a thief and a murderer. A woman who was branded. I'm speaking of Milady de Winter."

"If she has committed those crimes, she'll be punished," said the cardinal.

"She has been punished, Your Eminence. My friends and I captured her, tried her, and sentenced her to death."

D'Artagnan told him about Constance's death, the trial of Milady, and her execution.

When he had finished, the cardinal

said, "What you did was against the law. You will be tried, convicted, and executed."

"I think not, Your Eminence," d'Artagnan said with a smile. "Because I have had your permission for everything I have done."

"What do you mean?" Richelieu asked.

D'Artagnan handed him the letter Athos had taken from Milady. The cardinal took it and read out loud, "The bearer of this letter has acted under my orders and for the good of France. Richelieu."

He stood, lost in thought, twisting and untwisting the paper in his hands. Finally, he slowly tore up the letter. Then he picked up his pen and wrote something on a piece of parchment.

"I'm lost!" thought d'Artagnan. "He's writing out my death warrant."

"Here," the cardinal said, handing the parchment to d'Artagnan.

D'Artagnan looked at the parchment and gasped in surprise. "It's a commission as a lieutenant in the musketeers!" he cried.

"Yes," said the cardinal. "I've left a blank space for the name. You can write it in yourself."

D'Artagnan fell to his knees before the cardinal. "Thank you, Your Eminence," he said. "But I don't deserve this honor. I have three friends who are much more worthy of a commission than I am."

"Well, do what you like with the commission. But remember. It's to you that I give it," said the cardinal.

"I will never forget this honor, Your Eminence. You can be sure of that."

The cardinal turned and called out, "Rochefort!"

The count came into the room.

"Monsieur d'Artagnan is now my friend," the cardinal told Rochefort. "That means he is your friend, too. I want you to shake hands with each other and forget your quarrel."

Rochefort and d'Artagnan glared at each other. Then they shook hands quickly while the cardinal watched them closely.

They walked out of the room together.

"We can continue our quarrel another time," said Rochefort.

"Whenever you like," said d'Artagnan.

"We'll meet again soon," Rochefort promised.

Just then, the cardinal opened the door behind them. "What are you saying?" he asked suspiciously.

The two men smiled at each other. They shook hands again and bowed to His Eminence.

D'Artagnan left the house and walked over to his friends.

"We were beginning to worry," said Athos.

D'Artagnan told them what had happened between himself and the cardinal. Then he took the parchment from his pocket and held it out to Athos. "Take it, Athos. It rightly belongs to you."

Athos smiled warmly. "My dear friend," he said. "This commission is too much for a soldier like Athos. And it is too little for the Count de la Fère. You keep it. You have earned it."

D'Artagnan turned to Porthos. "Please take the commission, my friend. Think how good you will look in the uniform of a lieutenant!"

"I'd be happy to take it," said Porthos. "But I wouldn't have time to enjoy it. I have plans to marry a rich widow. So keep the commission, my friend. You deserve it."

"What about you, Aramis?" asked d'Artagnan. "You've earned this commission more than anyone because of your wisdom and your good advice. It should be yours. Will you take it?"

"No, my friend," said Aramis. "I've decided to resign from the musketeers and become a priest. Keep the commission, d'Artagnan. You'll be a brave and daring lieutenant."

"But I'll lose all my friends if I become an officer," cried d'Artagnan.

"That will never happen," said Athos. He wrote d'Artagnan's name on the blank line of the parchment. “Have you forgotten our motto?”

The four musketeers smiled at one another. Then they drew their swords and crossed them high above their heads. Together they shouted, “All for one, and one for all!”

Alexandre Dumas was born in France in 1802. He wrote several great novels and plays. Many of the characters in his stories were based on real people.

Dumas is best known for writing *The Count of Monte Cristo* and *The Three Musketeers*. Dumas later wrote several more books about d'Artagnan and his fearless friends, including *Twenty Years After* and *The Man in the Iron Mask*. Dumas died when he was sixty-eight years old.

Deborah Felder is the author of many books, including the Stepping Stones adaptation of *Anne of Green Gables*. She loves to travel, and one of her favorite things to do is visit the places she reads about in books. She and her husband live in Connecticut with their cat, Lily.

If you liked this thrilling adventure,
you won't want to miss . . .

by James Fenimore Cooper
adapted by Les Martin

Heyward moved back toward Natty. He took a paddle. Soon he picked up Natty's rhythm. The silence was broken only by the rippling water. Then came a distant roaring.

Heyward looked over the side. The water was swirling. Rocks jutted through white foam.

The roaring grew louder.

Heyward turned his eyes forward. He sucked in his breath.

A giant waterfall was dead ahead. The canoe was heading straight for it.

Fifty feet more and the waterfall would hit them. Crush them. Drown them all.

TREASURE ISLAND

by **Robert Louis Stevenson**
adapted by **Lisa Norby**

I scrambled onto the deck. Israel Hands lay nearby, alive but wounded.

"I am taking over the ship," I told him.

Mr. Hands looked up at me. "Very well, Captain Hawkins," he said. "I'll obey you. I have no choice."

For a few minutes I was so busy that I almost forgot that Mr. Hands was just pretending to be badly hurt. But all of a sudden something made me turn around. He had sneaked up behind me! He pulled out the knife. Then he charged.